AMANDA PIG
AND HER
BEST FRIEND
LOLLIPOP

Jean Van Leeuwen

PICTURES BY

ANN SCHWENINGER

SCHOLASTIC INC.
New York   Toronto   London   Auckland   Sydney
Mexico City   New Delhi   Hong Kong   Buenos Aires

For Elizabeth and Karen
J.V.L.

For Ron
A.S.

ISBN 0-439-61771-5

Text copyright © 1998 by Jean Van Leeuwen. Illustrations copyright © 1998 by Ann Schweninger. All rights reserved. Published by Scholastic Inc., 557 Broadway, New York, NY 10012, by arrangement with Puffin Books, a member of Penguin Group (USA) Inc. SCHOLASTIC and associated logos are trademarks and/or registered trademarks of Scholastic Inc.

12 11 10 9 8 7 6 5 4 3 2 1   4 5 6 7 8 9/0

Printed in the U.S.A.   23

First Scholastic printing, February 2004

The full-color artwork was prepared using carbon pencil, colored pencils, and watercolor washes. It was then color-separated and reproduced as red, blue, yellow, and black halftones.

CONTENTS

Whispers   5

The Babies   16

Lollipop's House   26

The Sleepover   36

WHISPERS

"This is the very best day,"

said Amanda.

"Lollipop is coming to play."

"You made up a poem!" said Mother.

"Yes, I did," said Amanda.

While she waited for Lollipop,
Amanda skipped rope.

"Today is the best day," she sang.

"Lollipop is coming to play."

But Lollipop did not come.

"Lollipop is late. I hate to wait,"

sang Amanda.

"Oops, it's another poem!"

Then, suddenly, there was Lollipop.

"This is my best friend, Lollipop,"

said Amanda.

"Hello, Lollipop," said Mother.

But Lollipop did not say anything.

"Let's play!" said Amanda.

She showed Lollipop her room

and all her toys and Sallie Rabbit.

"I have a rabbit too," said Lollipop.

"Her name is Gloria.

Next time I will bring her."

Amanda and Lollipop played School.

They played Build the Biggest City

in the Whole World.

"Would you girls like a snack?"

asked Mother.

Lollipop did not say anything.

But she whispered in Amanda's ear.

"Yes!" said Amanda.

They had milk and cookies.

"Would you like another cookie?"

asked Mother.

Lollipop whispered in Amanda's ear.

"Yes, please," said Amanda.

Mother whispered in Amanda's ear.

"Why won't Lollipop talk to me?"

"She is shy," whispered Amanda.

Amanda and Lollipop played Ballet.

They did pirouettes until

they got so dizzy, they both fell down.

"I bet you girls would like a drink,"

said Mother. "Grape or apple juice?"

Lollipop whispered in Amanda's ear.

"Apple," said Amanda.

With their juice they had lollipops.

"How did you know

Lollipop loves lollipops

more than anything?" asked Amanda.

"Oh, I just guessed," said Mother.

Amanda and Lollipop went outside.

They took turns on the swing.

"I swung so high,

my toes touched the sky,"

said Amanda.

"Hey, it's a poem again!"

"Let me try," said Lollipop.

She swung so high into the sky

that she fell off.

"Mother!" called Amanda.

Mother came running.

She picked up Lollipop.

"Where does it hurt?" she asked.

Lollipop did not say anything.

She was crying.

"Here?" said Mother.

She kissed Lollipop's elbow.

"Here?" She kissed her ear.

Lollipop whispered in Mother's ear.

"Oh, there!" said Mother.

She kissed Lollipop's knee.

"All better," Mother said.

And they both smiled.

THE BABIES

The next day

Lollipop brought her rabbit to play.

"Sallie," said Amanda, "this is Gloria.

Look, they like each other.

Maybe they will be best friends too."

"I know what," said Lollipop.

"Let's play that they are our babies."

"Good idea," said Amanda.

They dressed their babies.

"It is cool today," said Lollipop.

"I think they will need sweaters."

Then they fed them.

"Sallie loves bananas," said Amanda.

"So does Gloria," said Lollipop.

"But she is a little fussy today.

She is teething, you know."

Then they got the babies
ready for a walk.

"We better change their diapers first,"
said Lollipop. "And put on their hats."

"You know a lot about babies,"

said Amanda.

"I have a baby sister," said Lollipop.

"Eat and sleep, eat and sleep.

That's all they ever do."

"Sallie is awake now," said Amanda.

"Look, Sallie. See the pretty leaves."

"And the bird," said Lollipop.

"And Oliver," said Amanda.

"Do you want to play Jump in

All the Leaf Piles?" asked Oliver.

Lollipop whispered in Amanda's ear.

"No," said Amanda.

"We have to take care of our babies."

They walked some more.

"Uh-oh," said Lollipop.

"Gloria is crying."

"What is the matter?" asked Amanda.

"It is her teeth again," said Lollipop.

"But she likes it when I sing to her.

'Hush, little baby, don't you cry.

Teeth are good to eat with.'"

"That was almost a poem," said Amanda.

Oliver jumped out of a leaf pile.

"Want to play Hide-and-Seek

in the leaves?" he asked.

Lollipop whispered in Amanda's ear.

"One of our babies is sick,"

said Amanda. "Don't bother us."

"I think it is naptime," said Lollipop.

They wheeled the babies home.

They made a bed for them

in the big chair

and tucked them in nice and cozy.

"Now do you want to play?"

Oliver took a great big jump

into the big chair.

"Watch out!" cried Amanda.

"Our babies!" said Lollipop.

"You squashed them."

"Sorry," said Oliver.

Amanda and Lollipop hugged the babies.

Amanda whispered in Lollipop's ear.

"You yelled at Oliver.

Maybe you're not shy anymore."

"Maybe not," said Lollipop.

And they rocked their babies to sleep.

"Rock-a-bye, babies," they sang,

"in the treetops."

LOLLIPOP'S HOUSE

Lollipop had the best house.

She had a purple room.

"I love purple," said Amanda.

"I painted it all by myself,"

said Lollipop. "With my father."

She had bunk beds. And a whole closet

full of dress-up clothes.

And best of all, she had her baby sister.

Lulu was her name.

"Baby sisters are much better

than big brothers," said Amanda.

"Can we play with her?"

"Later," said Lollipop.

"Now she has to have lunch."

Amanda and Lollipop played games.

They played Ballet on the couch.

"Your mother lets you?" said Amanda.

"Sure," said Lollipop.

That was another good thing

about Lollipop's house.

"Can we play with Lulu yet?"

asked Amanda.

"Now she is having her nap,"

said Lollipop.

Amanda and Lollipop played Cooking.

"You can use real food?" said Amanda.

"Of course," said Lollipop.

That was another great thing

about Lollipop's house.

They mixed up peanut butter
and marshmallows and applesauce.
"Mmm, yummy," said Amanda.

They mixed up mustard and jam
and cinnamon and pickles.
"Disgusting!" said Lollipop.

They went to the kitchen to clean up.

There was Lulu, having a snack.

"What did I tell you?" said Lollipop.

"Eat and sleep, eat and sleep."

"Is that really all she can do?"

asked Amanda.

"Well," said Lollipop, "she can play
Peekaboo. And throw things.
And she is learning to talk. She says
'Bye-bye' and 'Papa' and 'Mama.'
But she can't say 'Lollipop.'"
"Let's teach her," said Amanda.
She held up a lollipop.
"Peeky-boo," said Lulu.

"No, no," said Amanda. "Lollipop."

"Googy googy gaga," said Lulu.

"See what I mean?" said Lollipop.

She took a lick of her lollipop.

"Look, Lulu," she said. "Lolly. Pop."

"Oopy doop," said Lulu.

"I give up," said Lollipop.

It was time to go home.

"Don't worry," said Amanda.

"Next time I come to play,

we will give her another lesson.

Good-bye, everyone."

"Bye, Amanda," said Lollipop.

"Come again," said Lollipop's mother.

"Mamba," said Lulu.

"Did you hear that?" said Amanda.

"She said my name!"

"Bye-bye, Mamba," said Lulu.

And that was the very best thing about Lollipop's house.

THE SLEEPOVER

Amanda loved Lollipop's house.

She loved it so much,

she wished she didn't have to go home.

"I know what!" said Lollipop.

"Tomorrow you can sleep over."

"Can I? Can I? Can I?" begged Amanda.

"Are you sure you want to?" said Father.

"Yes, yes, yes, yes, yes!" said Amanda.

So she packed her little suitcase

and went to sleep at Lollipop's house.

She and Lollipop played with Lulu.

They played Peekaboo
and Pick Up Lulu's Toys.

"Say 'Lollipop,'" said Amanda.

"Lollipop, Lollipop, LOLLIPOP!"

"Olli-op," said Lulu at last.

"She did it!" said Lollipop. "Hooray!"

They had popcorn and root-beer floats.

Lollipop's house had super snacks.

Then it was time for bed.

"Do you want the top bunk

or the bottom?" asked Lollipop.

"The top," said Amanda.

"It's like sleeping in a tree."

Lollipop's mother tucked them in.

"Now," said Lollipop,

"we can talk all night."

They played What Is Your Favorite?

"What is your favorite ice cream?"

asked Lollipop.

"Strawberry," said Amanda.

"What is your favorite color?"

Lollipop did not say anything.

"Lollipop?" said Amanda.

"I can't believe it. She is asleep."

Amanda tried to go to sleep.

But her eyes kept popping open.

It felt strange to be up so high.

If she moved, she might fall out.

And what were all those funny shadows?

Maybe one of them was a monster.

Squeak! went something at the window.

"What was that?" whispered Amanda.

Squeak! Tap, tap, tap!

A monster's claws

were scratching at the glass.

Amanda hid way down under the covers.

She hugged Sallie Rabbit tight.

"What is the matter," she said,

"that makes your teeth chatter?

That was a scary poem."

She wished Oliver was there.

He would say, "Don't be dumb.

There is no such thing as monsters."

Father would chase the monster away.

"I want to go home," whispered Amanda.

She waited until the monster was quiet.

Then very carefully she climbed down

and tiptoed out of Lollipop's room.

The house was dark.

Everything was still.

Amanda found the telephone.

"Hello," said Father's sleepy voice.

"I changed my mind," said Amanda.

"I don't want to sleep over."

"But I am asleep," said Father.

"And it is raining outside."

"Please?" said Amanda.

"I will be right there," said Father.

They walked home in the rain.

"The bed was too high," said Amanda.

"And it was too dark.

And there was a monster at the window."

"It was only the rain," said Father.

"Maybe," said Amanda.

"But you know what?

I like Lollipop's house in the daytime.

But at night I like my own house."